WHY US?

THE SILENT BATTLE WITHIN

PANKAJ MADHUKAR

Contents

Preface   vii

  1. The Park   1

  2. The Diary   4

  3. Bonds Beyond The Benches   8

  4. The Deer Park Plan   12

  5. Arunima's Flashback   18

  6. The Big Revelation   21

  7. Guilt And Reflection   24

  8. Unraveling The Mystery   26

  9. Mind Harmony Clinic   28

10. Life Is Not Easy   30

Preface

Life, with its capricious twists and turns, unfolds narratives that echo with tales of joy, sorrow, and unyielding resilience. In the ensuing chapters, we embark on a profound exploration of Vihaan's world—a realm where the boundaries between reality and imagination waver, familial bonds are tested, and the hushed murmurs of mental health challenges reverberate.

These chapters unfurl as a poignant journey through the labyrinth of Vihaan's emotions, providing readers with a glimpse into the depths of his heart. From the simple anticipation of a park rendezvous with a newfound friend to the stark realization that his family treads uncharted territories of illness and well-being, Vihaan's odyssey prompts contemplation on themes of love, sacrifice, and the relentless quest for understanding.

As the narrative unfolds, it introduces characters whose lives intersect with Vihaan's, each carrying their unique burdens and joys. Through the prism of shared experiences, the story navigates the intricacies of human relationships, scrutinizing the essence of familial bonds and the resilience demanded when life takes unforeseen detours.

The emotional tapestry woven within these pages transcends Vihaan's singular experience. It extends beyond the confines of a park bench, delving into the hearts of readers who may discover echoes of their own struggles, triumphs, and reflections. Vihaan's journey, from the hopeful anticipation of a family outing to the shattering revelations reshaping his reality, serves as a mirror reflecting the intricate hues of the human spirit.

In the quietude of Vihaan's solitude, the echoes of his story beckon us to contemplate the fragility of mental health, the challenges confronted by families, and the profound resilience that blossoms in adversity.

Moreover, this narrative serves as a poignant reflection of Vihaan's parents, whose states of being intertwine with his own, creating a tapestry woven with the shared complexities of familial bonds and the silent battles faced by each individual.

The Park

The worn-out bus rumbled to a halt, its brakes squealing in reluctant harmony with the reluctant Vihaan inside. The driver turned in his weathered seat, his eyes meeting the boy's with a mix of sympathy and understanding.

"Here's your stop, kiddo," the driver called out, the words carrying an unspoken acknowledgment of the boy's reluctance to disembark. The doors creaked open, revealing the boy's destination – his home.

A heavy sigh escaped the boy's lips, his shoulders slumping with the weight of unspoken burdens. The world outside seemed to lose its luster as he unwillingly dragged his feet towards the exit. The bus, a vessel of routine, had betrayed his desire to delay the inevitable return.

Reluctantly, he stepped down onto the familiar sidewalk, the ground beneath him feeling less like solid concrete and more like the quicksand of responsibility. The driver, with a nod of understanding, closed the door behind him. The engine roared back to life, a metallic growl that seemed to mock the boy's reluctance.

As the bus pulled away, leaving the boy standing on the threshold of his home, his gaze lingered on the receding vehicle. He felt like a solitary figure in a story he didn't want to unfold. With a heavy heart, he trudged towards the front door, each step echoing the internal conflict of a boy who longed for freedom in a place that felt more like a cage.

The weight of the day lingered as Vihaan entered his home. True to the mundane routine, he found no warm welcome from his mom, only a note affixed to the refrigerator with the familiar magnet his eyes had come to resent. The message conveyed her absence, the house echoing with a silence that seemed to amplify his solitude.

The note read, " I'll be taking Ahaan outside. I've prepared some food for you in the refrigerator. Please have a meal, and at 5, go to your soccer classes. I'll be back home by the time you return."

His appetite lost its appeal in the face of loneliness, the house mocking him with its emptiness. To combat the silent taunts, he turned to Alexa, pleading for a distraction. He requested Alexa to activate the radio. An akon's song began there.

Lonely, I'm Mr. Lonely
I have nobody for my own
I'm so lonely, I'm Mr. Lonely
I have nobody for my own
I am so lonely.

As the lyrics echoed, the pangs of loneliness pushed Vihaan further to escape the confines of his home. Without bothering to eat, he changed into his soccer gear and hastily left for his class. The soccer field became his refuge, a place where the ball became a temporary companion, and the rhythm of the game eased the ache in his heart. He yearned for time to stand still in those moments of solace.

When the soccer class concluded, rather than heading home, he diverted to a nearby park. Seated on a bench, he tried to make sense of the whirlwind of emotions swirling within him. Lost in thought, he unintentionally became aware of a girl who chose the bench beside him. Her presence was palpable, and a subtle energy suggested she desired conversation.

Part of him wished she would leave, but something prompted him to break the silence. "Hi, I'm Vihaan," he uttered, a hesitant bridge into a realm beyond his solitude.

The girl's voice resonated with warmth as she greeted, "Hi, I'm Arunima!" A profound silence settled in. Though Vihaan harbored a curiosity about her name, unfamiliar and intriguing, he chose to keep his inquiry unspoken. It felt almost inconceivable to him that, three years since the birth of his younger brother Ahaan, he remained unnoticed and unloved. In the eyes of his parents, it seemed as though he simply didn't exist. Despite this emotional turmoil, a peculiar sense of connection with the girl beside him emerged.

After a while, Arunima acknowledged the passing time, mentioning that it was time for her to head home. With a gentle concern, she advised Vihaan, "You should also go home; your parents will be worried!"

In a hushed tone, Vihaan admitted, "No one is worried for me." Nevertheless, he gathered himself and left for home, the weight of solitude lingering in his every step.

The Diary

Upon returning home, Vihaan found his mother engrossed in playful interaction with Ahaan. Eager to join the familial warmth, he approached, and his mother greeted him with affection, inquiring about his day. Before Vihaan could respond, Ahaan requested water, prompting his mother to swiftly head to the kitchen.

Upon her return with water, she repeated her question to Vihaan. However, the doorbell interrupted the moment, announcing the arrival of his father. Excitedly exchanging greetings with his father, Vihaan observed the seemingly more genuine connection between his father and Ahaan. Sensing Vihaan's emotions, his father invited him into his lap, momentarily bringing joy to Vihaan, though a lingering belief persisted that his father favored Ahaan. Following his father's arrival, his mother's focus shifted towards his father, and his response to his mother's question lingered in his heart. He yearned to confide in his mother, sharing the events of the day with her, including his encounter with Arunima. Unfortunately, his mother was preoccupied and didn't have the time, being deeply engrossed in her own busyness.

Post-dinner, Vihaan's father embarked on his customary evening walk. Vihaan retired to his room for the night, while Ahaan slept with their mother. With a penchant for journaling, Vihaan proceeded to retrieve his diary. In doing so, he noticed an older diary and opted to read its contents instead. He flipped the page of the diary and it read:

Dear Diary,

Guess what?! Today was the most amazing day ever! Mom and Dad told me the best news, and I can't stop smiling! You won't believe it—I'm going to have a little brother! A real-life, tiny buddy to play with and share secrets. How cool is that?

This morning, Mom and Dad called me into the living room. I was wondering what was going on because they had these big smiles on their faces. And then they told me the incredible news – "You're going to be a big brother!"

I couldn't believe my ears. A mix of excitement and happiness bubbled up inside me. It's like getting the best birthday present ever, but even better! I'm going to teach him everything I know, like how to build the tallest LEGO towers and the best hiding spots in hide-and-seek. Oh, and of course, the secret handshake only big brothers and little brothers can have.

I rushed to Mom and gave her the biggest hug. She looked so happy, and her eyes were all shiny with joy. I could tell this is a special moment for our family.

I spent the rest of the day thinking about what it will be like. I imagined holding my baby brother for the first time and telling him all about the adventures we're going to have together. I even thought about the cool superhero names we could have as a dynamic duo.

Tonight, I'm going to dream about all the fun we're going to have as brothers. I can't wait to meet him and show him the world.

Best day ever!

He flipped and skipped few pages and landed on the below page:

Dear Diary,

Today was one of the scariest days of my life. Something happened to Ahaan, my little brother, and it shook our world. This morning, he became unconscious, and Mom and Dad rushed him to the hospital. Aunt Vini came to take care of me, but my thoughts were constantly with Ahaan.

The whole day felt like an eternity. I kept praying to God, begging Him not to take away my brother. I felt a knot in my stomach, and my heart was heavy with worry. Every passing minute felt like an hour, and I just wanted to see Ahaan safe and sound.

Finally, late in the night, Mom and Dad came back from the hospital. Their faces looked different, and I couldn't tell if it was from the exhaustion of a long day or the emotional stress they went through. My heart pounded as I waited to hear about Ahaan.

When they opened the door, my eyes searched for Ahaan. And there he was—weak but back on his feet. I felt a rush of relief and happiness. He looked at me and called me "bhaiya" with a weak smile. That single word made my day, my week, my everything. I hugged him tightly, thankful that he was back and on the road to recovery.

I don't think I've ever been so grateful for anything in my life. Today taught me the value of family, the fragility of life, and the power of hope. I'll cherish every moment with Ahaan, grateful for the chance to be his big brother.

Feeling blessed,

Closing the diary, he engaged in introspection. "Slowly, everything changed from that moment onward," he whispered to himself. Shortly after, he drifted into sleep. His father returned from his walk, entered Vihaan's room, gently kissed his forehead, and turned off the light.

CHAPTER THREE

Bonds beyond the benches

The following day, after his soccer classes, Vihaan returned to the park with the hope of encountering Arunima once again. Though their interactions had been brief, he felt an unexplained connection with her and yearned to meet her again. Seated on the same bench, he scanned the surroundings, but the evening's darkness began to envelop the park, and Arunima was nowhere in sight.

Just as Vihaan resigned himself to the fading light, a voice interrupted his thoughts. "Vihaan, is it you?" Turning around, he discovered Arunima standing behind him. Overwhelmed with surprise and joy, he stood up and approached her.

"Hey, how are you?" Vihaan managed to utter, still processing the unexpected reunion.

"I am good. How are you? At least you look better than last evening," Arunima remarked, noting the change in Vihaan's demeanor.

Vihaan nodded in agreement but found himself at a loss for words. When Arunima suggested a walk, he willingly agreed, and they strolled together through the park.

During their conversation, Arunima shared that she had informed her mother about Vihaan. This revelation touched Vihaan deeply, and he whispered a grateful acknowledgment. However, when Vihaan expressed his perception of Arunima's fortunate relationship with her parents, Arunima, puzzled, questioned why he felt that way.

Vihaan hesitated but eventually opened up. He explained how his family dynamics changed after the arrival of his younger brother, Ahaan. The newfound attention and time everyone dedicated to Ahaan had shifted the family dynamics, and Vihaan began to share the challenges he faced in this new reality.

Arunima gazed at Vihaan with genuine curiosity, her eyes reflecting a mixture of understanding and compassion. Breaking the silence, she inquired, "How old is your brother?"

Vihaan's response was swift, "He completed four, last month."

Arunima acknowledged this with a warm smile, but as the conversation continued, Vihaan's words took on a more introspective tone. "It's not that I don't love my brother. He is the best thing that has happened in our family. I feel like laughing with his smile, tears roll over my eyes when he is sad." His words conveyed a deep affection for Ahaan, revealing the genuine love and care he held for his younger sibling.

However, the atmosphere shifted as Vihaan delved into his emotions, expressing a sentiment that weighed heavily on his heart. "However, I do not know why these days, at home, I feel like I don't belong there. Everyone is there, but still, I feel a sense of emptiness surrounding me."

In these words, Vihaan laid bare a profound inner struggle. Despite the love he felt for his family and the joy derived from Ahaan's presence, a palpable sense of emptiness pervaded his thoughts. It hinted at a complex emotional journey, one where the dynamics of familial relationships and personal identity intertwined, leaving Vihaan searching for a place where he could find solace and a sense of belonging.

Arunima, stirred by Vihaan's heartfelt admission, found herself at a loss for words. The weight of his internal conflicts resonated with her, and in that moment, words seemed inadequate. Instinctively, she reached out and gently held his hand, offering a silent gesture of empathy and support.

Vihaan continued to share the complexities of his emotions.

"You know, I have been complaining about a headache for the last three days, but my dad told me that he would take me to the doctor over the weekend as he will have to take leave from the office. But today, Ahaan had a minor fever, Daddy took leave and took Ahaan to the hospital. These incidents further boost my belief that I am not as important," Vihaan confided.

Tears welled up in his eyes, his voice weighed down by the emotional burden he carried.

Arunima, realizing the depth of Vihaan's struggle, gently asked, "Did you talk about these to your parents?"

"When will I tell them? They do not have time! Before you, the only other place where I vented my feelings is my diary," Vihaan admitted.

Sharing his feelings seemed to lift a weight off his shoulders, yet he couldn't shake the internal conflict of speaking about his parents and little brother to a stranger.

As the evening enveloped them in contemplative silence, Vihaan, lost in his thoughts, was brought back to reality by Arunima's practical words. "It is very late now; we should go home."

These words acted as a gentle reminder that, even in the midst of sharing his deepest feelings, life continued, and responsibilities awaited.

Before parting ways, Vihaan, expressing gratitude for the unexpected connection, looked at Arunima and said, "Thank you."

Those simple words carried the weight of unspoken emotions, acknowledging the comfort and understanding he found in this chance encounter. The night embraced them as they went their separate ways, leaving behind a lingering sense of shared vulnerability and newfound connection.

The deer park plan

Today is Saturday, and Vihaan's schedule is packed with various classes—keyboard, drawing, and karate. Despite the anticipated hustle, Vihaan eagerly counts down the hours, eager for the day to end and his visit to the park. The excitement stems from the anticipation of meeting his newfound friend, Arunima. Although Vihaan isn't sure about the specifics of their conversation, what matters most to him is the joy he experiences in Arunima's company, and that thought alone brings him happiness.

As the day progresses and Vihaan completes all his classes, he makes his way to the park, finding solace on the familiar bench. However, the atmosphere changes when Arunima fails to show up. Vihaan patiently waits until 8 PM, but disappointment sets in as she doesn't arrive. With a heavy heart, he reluctantly leaves the park and heads back home, grappling with the uncertainty of why Arunima didn't join him.

Questions linger in Vihaan's mind—Was she unwell? Did she have other commitments? Or did unforeseen circumstances keep her away? The ambiguity adds to his sense of disappointment, and he contemplates various scenarios in an attempt to understand Arunima's absence.

As he reaches home, Vihaan's parents express concern, noticing his late return. Yet, they refrain from probing, trusting Vihaan's judgment. After a quiet dinner, Vihaan's dad surprises him with plans to visit a nearby deer park, momentarily diverting his attention from Arunima's absence. The prospect of a family outing, a rare occurrence since Ahaan's birth, reignites Vihaan's excitement, temporarily overshadowing the earlier disappointment.

The following morning, Vihaan wakes up with renewed anticipation, searching for his dad to learn the day's plans. Unable to find him, he assumes his father is out for work. Vihaan completes his breakfast, awaiting the unfolding events of the day in eager anticipation. The air is thick with silence until the doorbell rings.

Expecting his dad, Vihaan opens the door only to find Aunty Vini. The unexpected sight of Aunty Vini instantly signals a shift in the anticipated agenda. Vihaan senses that his eagerly awaited family outing might be in jeopardy as Aunty Vini, a middle-aged lady known for her chronic backache, typically refrains from participating in outdoor activities. The very thought of the change of plans makes him frustrated. But despite his inner frustration, Vihaan manages to greet Aunty Vini with a polite demeanor, masking his disappointment.

Closing the door behind him, Vihaan retreats to his room, where conflicting emotions stir within him. On one hand, he understands Aunty Vini's physical limitations and respects her condition. On the other hand, the prospect of an outdoor excursion being replaced with an ordinary day at home disappoints him.

In his room, Vihaan contemplates the situation, wrestling with his feelings of frustration and understanding. He wonders if there could be alternative plans or activities that accommodate Aunty Vini's condition while still providing an enjoyable experience for everyone.

As the afternoon progresses, Vihaan, still hopeful for an unexpected turn of events, remains in his room, perhaps engaging in activities to distract himself from the changed circumstances. The house, once filled with the anticipation of a family outing, now holds an air of uncertainty and subdued disappointment. The doorbell, which initially brought the unexpected news of Aunty Vini's presence, remains silent, leaving Vihaan to navigate his emotions and the altered plans in solitude.

Frustration and disappointment lingering, Vihaan inadvertently succumbs to the emotional weight of the day. In his room, the swirling thoughts about the altered plans and the absence of the eagerly anticipated family outing weigh heavily on his mind. Despite his attempts to engage in activities, the emotional toll leads Vihaan into an unexpected nap. The fatigue from the day's events and the emotional rollercoaster eventually lull him into a restless sleep.

As Vihaan dozes off, time slips away, and the atmosphere within the house remains hushed. The doorbell, once the harbinger of unexpected changes, stays silent, contributing to the quiet ambiance that envelops the space.

Upon waking up, Vihaan finds himself disoriented. The room, dimly lit, suggests that evening has settled in. The realization dawns on him that the house is unusually still. A sense of unease sets in as he navigates the rooms, seeking the presence of his parents and Ahaan.

To his surprise, the house remains empty—no sign of his dad, mom, or Ahaan. The absence of their familiar presence amplifies Vihaan's confusion and concern. Aunty Vini, who was previously sleeping in the guest bedroom, now adds to the quietude that engulfs the home.

Vihaan's search extends to every corner of the house, yet no one is in sight. Anxiety creeps in as he contemplates the possibilities. Were they delayed in their plans? Did they go out without waking him up? Questions swarm his mind, adding to the heightened sense of uncertainty that defines this unexpected turn of events.

Thirsty and perplexed, Vihaan heads to the kitchen to quench his thirst. As he opens the refrigerator door, he notices a note carefully placed within. His heart skips a beat as he reads the words penned by his mom. "Vihaan, Daddy and I are going out with Ahaan, we may be late. Aunty Vini will take care of you, do not trouble her. We may be late."

The words hit Vihaan with a sudden wave of emotion. The realization that his family had left without waking him, even for a seemingly special outing, leaves him feeling a profound sense of isolation. The message, intended to reassure him, instead cements the feeling that they didn't consider him a crucial part of their plans. Saddened by this re-realization, Vihaan grapples with a mix of emotions — disappointment, loneliness, and a touch of abandonment.

In an attempt to find solace, Vihaan rushes to the park, hoping that the familiar surroundings and the tranquility of the outdoor space will help ease the emotional turbulence within him. As he approaches the park, he notices Arunima already seated on the bench, almost as if she had been waiting for him.

As Vihaan catches sight of Arunima in the park, a tumult of emotions engulfs him. A solitary tear escapes his eye, tracing a path down his cheek. The conflicting feelings within him create an emotional haze, making it challenging for Vihaan to decipher whether the tear is an expression of joy at seeing Arunima or a manifestation of the pain stemming from his parents' decision to exclude him from their plans and take only Ahaan along. Vihaan sat beside her, his emotions echoing loudly through the silence. Unsure of what to say, Arunima chose to remain quiet, allowing him the space he needed. After a moment, Vihaan took a deep breath and finally spoke.

Vihaan: Arunima, I just can't shake off the feeling that my parents don't care about me. They left without telling me about their plans, and it hurts.

Vihaan continued, narrating the entire sequence of events that unfolded throughout the day. His words carried the weight of disappointment and confusion, painting a vivid picture of his emotional journey. Arunima listened with empathy, absorbing every detail. After a while, she spoke.

Arunima: Vihaan, I understand it's tough, but maybe there's a reason they had to leave. Before jumping to conclusions, try to talk with them. Don't let assumptions cloud your thoughts.

Vihaan: But what if they just don't care? What if I'm not as important to them as Ahaan is?

Arunima: Vihaan, I've been there. Trust me, parents always love their children, but sometimes they might not express it in the way we expect. Instead of assuming the worst, have a conversation with them. Ask them directly about your concerns.

Vihaan expressed his frustration, *"It's just hard, Arunima. I waited the whole day to spend time with them, and they left for some plans without me. It feels like I'm not a priority."*

The words hung in the air, laden with the weight of his emotions. Arunima, recognizing the depth of his feelings, offered a comforting presence, ready to support him through the turmoil.

Arunima: I get it. It's tough when expectations don't match reality. Patience is crucial. Remember, there's a reason behind everything. Share your feelings with them when they return but give them a chance to explain too.

Vihaan: You think they'll listen?

Arunima: Absolutely. Parents care deeply for their children, but sometimes they may not realize how their actions affect us. Communicating openly will help bridge that gap and let them know how you feel.

Vihaan: I am not sure. Have you ever felt like your parents didn't love you?

Arunima: Oh, Vihaan, I've been through similar struggles. When I was really small, my parents were always busy with work, and I always felt neglected. It seemed like their jobs were more important than me.

Vihaan: Really? But they do love you, right?

Arunima: Absolutely, Vihaan. It took a difficult situation, much like yours, for them to realize the importance of expressing their love. Your parents love you; they just might not be showing it in the way you expect.

As Arunima shared, her eyes sparkled with memories of a time when love found its way through life's challenges.

CHAPTER FIVE

Arunima's flashback

Arunima's mind wandered back to the tender years of her childhood, where every day felt like an eternity at the daycare. My parents, both engrossed in their jobs, would leave me behind, tears welling up in my eyes as I clung to the hope that one day, they'd choose me over work.

Arunima: "Mom, please don't go today. Stay with me."

There were days when all I wanted was to play hide and seek with my mother, to bask in the melodies of her laughter, and share tears together. However, it felt like her job held a higher priority, drowning out the simple joys of our shared moments.

It wasn't just the daycare that stood as a barrier. Even when my parents returned home, exhaustion etched lines on their faces. I'd wait the entire day, my heart eager to spill the stories I had woven, the rhymes I had learned, and simply to play with them. Yet, when they finally returned, the kitchen and household chores absorbed their attention, leaving me stranded in a sea of unfulfilled yearning.

Arunima: "I just wanted them to be present, to share in my joys and sorrows. But they were always so tired."

Their weariness became a wall between us, a wall that left me yearning for their undivided attention. The house echoed with the silence of unspoken desires, the rhythm of my heartbeat syncing with the ache of longing for a connection that seemed elusive.

One day, a fever gripped me, but even that couldn't alter the routine.

Arunima: "Mom, I'm not feeling well today. Can you stay with me?"

Mom: "Oh sweetheart, it's just a little fever. I've brought your medicines, and you'll feel better soon. I'll be back to pick you up in the evening."

A part of her heart, heavy with concern, seemed to linger with me as she handed over the medicines. I wished she could keep that part of her heart with me, a balm for my lonely moments at the daycare.

Arunima: "But I want you to stay, Mom."

Mom: "I wish I could, Aru, but I have to go to work. Be a brave girl, and I'll be back soon. Love you!"

Her words were a mixture of reassurance and longing, a delicate balance between the responsibilities she carried and the desire to comfort her ailing child. As she left, the daycare's walls seemed to close in, echoing with the distant sounds of children playing and my muffled cries for the comfort that only a mother could provide.

Arunima (waking up in the hospital): "Where am I?"

My eyes met hers, red and swollen from countless tears. The overwhelming emotions emanating from her told a story of a night filled with worry and heartache.

Arunima: "Where's Dad?"

Mom: "He's outside, waiting. He's been so strong for you, Aru."

Arunima: "I don't want to go back to the daycare, Mom."

In that vulnerable moment, my mother made a choice that altered the course of our lives—she sacrificed her job. It was a decision that, at the time, I couldn't fathom. But now, looking back, I realize the depth of that sacrifice, the love that transcended the demands of a career.

Arunima: "I didn't realize then how difficult it was for Mom. I was so stubborn."

As the realization dawned upon me, my heart swelled with gratitude and remorse. How could I have been so blind to the silent sacrifices of the people who loved me unconditionally?

This incident, etched in the canvas of my childhood, was just one of many that compelled me to reevaluate my understanding of my parents' love. It was a love that went beyond words, a love that I yearned for in the echoing hallways of the daycare.

Arunima: "I just wanted to be with them, to feel their love and warmth. I didn't realize how much they loved me until much later."

CHAPTER SIX

The big revelation

Vihaan was deeply moved by Arunima's heartfelt story. As he walked homeward, he contemplated how he would express his own yearning for love to his parents. The weight of unspoken emotions lingered in his steps, and the journey home became a rehearsal of the conversations he wished to have.

Upon entering his home, an unusual tension hung in the air, and he found his parents sitting in the living room, their faces etched with concern. It was a sight unfamiliar to Vihaan, and the absence of Ahaan intensified the surreal atmosphere. His mother's distressed state was particularly unsettling, as she rarely let Ahaan out of her sight.

Vihaan approached them, a knot of worry tightening in his stomach. He inquired about the situation, but his mother, on the verge of tears, struggled to find words. Witnessing his mother cry for the first-time left Vihaan feeling helpless. His usual instinct to seek her attention clashed with the reality of her sorrow.

Vihaan: "Mom, what happened? Where's Ahaan?"

His mother's tears were a poignant contrast to the love he had always sought from her. The conflicting emotions within him mirrored the turmoil in the room. The urge to join his mother in tears battled with his father's plea for composure.

Vihaan's father intervened, urging his wife not to cry and redirecting their focus to Ahaan. The mystery surrounding Ahaan's absence added to Vihaan's confusion, leaving him perplexed about the unfolding situation.

They asked Vihaan to accompany them to the hospital, their voices tinged with fear. Without uttering a word, Vihaan followed them. The car ride to the hospital was fraught with a heavy silence, interrupted only by the muffled sobs of his mother. Vihaan, sensing the gravity of the situation, mustered the courage to voice the question that hung heavily in the air.

Vihaan: "What happened to Ahaan? Where is he?"

His father, with a heavy sigh, began to unravel the story, taking Vihaan back to a couple of years ago when Ahaan first fell unconscious.

Father: "Do you remember when Ahaan fainted a couple of years back? That's when everything changed. We found out he has a disease called Krabbe. It was the first time we heard of it, and we didn't fully grasp the severity until the doctor said he had only two years left."

The weight of the revelation settled heavily on Vihaan, as he grasped the magnitude of the situation. His parents, devastated by the prognosis, had been silently battling the sorrow and fear that loomed over them. Vihaan's mother, in particular, had become increasingly absorbed in Ahaan's care, unwittingly creating a growing emotional distance.

Father: "Today, while you were sleeping, Ahaan lost consciousness again. We rushed him to the hospital, and there wasn't time to inform you."

As the car halted outside the hospital, Vihaan's heart raced, anticipating the unknown. An overwhelming sense of dread mixed with hope swirled within him. Vihaan anxiously asked if Ahaan was okay, his father offering a glimmer of reassurance.

Father: "He's stable for now. He wants to see you."

Initially hesitant to share this burden with Vihaan, his parents had yielded to the Aunt Vini's insistence. The truth, heavy with sorrow and the impending loss, hung in the air as they entered the hospital, bracing themselves for the emotional tumult that awaited them.

Guilt and Reflection

As Vihaan rushed towards the patient's ward, a whirlwind of conflicting emotions engulfed his heart. Guilt consumed him, a bitter realization that jealousy had momentarily clouded his love for his little brother. Instead of cherishing Ahaan's innocent words, Vihaan had yearned for his own stories to be heard by their parents. This self-awareness weighed heavily on him.

Simultaneously, anger flared towards an elusive higher power – a furious questioning of why Ahaan, a mere child, had to face such a cruel fate. In the same breath, a fleeting sense of relief washed over Vihaan as he saw Ahaan sleeping peacefully, temporarily allaying the storm within.

Yet, the relief was ephemeral, quickly replaced by the looming fear of Ahaan departing their world prematurely, a fear that gripped Vihaan's heart with an unrelenting intensity. The cacophony of emotions threatened to overwhelm him, leaving his mind on the brink of chaos.

However, as Vihaan gazed upon his slumbering brother, innocence personified, a silent promise unfolded within him. He vowed to himself that henceforth, he would actively participate in caring for Ahaan, sharing the responsibilities with their parents. The realization of being the elder son dawned upon him, a newfound sense of duty and protection settling in.

As Vihaan lingered at the threshold of the PICU (Pediatric Intensive Care Unit), a palpable reluctance clung to him. The sterile scent of disinfectant and the hum of medical machinery formed a dissonant backdrop to his tumultuous emotions. His gaze lingered on Ahaan, the frail figure in the hospital bed, surrounded by monitors that blinked with rhythmic precision.

The doctor, with a compassionate yet firm tone, reiterated, "I'm sorry, but we need to limit visitors in the PICU for now. It's in the best interest of the patient."

Vihaan hesitated, caught between the powerful desire to stay by Ahaan's side and the grim reality that he had to yield to the medical protocol. As he exchanged a lingering look with his parents, the unsaid words hung heavy in the air, a silent agreement forged through shared concern.

"I want to stay with Ahaan," Vihaan mumbled, his voice betraying a mix of determination and vulnerability.

His father, placing a comforting hand on Vihaan's shoulder, spoke with a gentle reassurance, "We all want to, beta, but the doctor knows what's best. Let's give Ahaan the space he needs to recover."

Reluctantly, Vihaan took a step back, tearing his gaze away from Ahaan. The room seemed to echo with unspoken emotions and the rhythmic beeping of medical equipment. As they exited, the heavy door closed behind them, muffling the sounds of the PICU and encapsulating the intensity of the moment.

CHAPTER EIGHT

Unraveling the mystery

Ahaan returned home after spending two days in the hospital, and Vihaan, eager to bring joy to his little brother, dedicated the entire day to creating colorful drawings and playful paper toys. The room echoed with Ahaan's delighted laughter as Vihaan presented his artistic creations, hoping to drown the recent somber memories in the warmth of sibling affection.

As the clock ticked towards 5 o'clock, a gentle reminder from his mother indicated that Vihaan's soccer class awaited him. He hesitated, expressing his reluctance to leave his brother's side, but his mother, with a reassuring smile, convinced him that it was okay to attend his soccer class.

The soccer field, usually a place of joy and camaraderie, felt somewhat different for Vihaan that evening. His mind, preoccupied with thoughts of Ahaan and the recent family ordeal, struggled to find the usual enthusiasm. Yet, determined to maintain a sense of normalcy, Vihaan participated in the class.

Post-soccer, with gratitude and the need for emotional solace in mind, Vihaan decided to visit the park. Arunima, his newfound confidante, crossed his thoughts. He wanted to express his gratitude, share the challenges his family was facing, and find solace in their unique bond.

Upon reaching the park, urgency fueled Vihaan's steps. In the dimming twilight, he spotted Arunima leaving through a diagonal exit gate. Desperate to catch her attention, Vihaan called out her name. Arunima turned, briefly acknowledging his presence, but hurried away without stopping. Vihaan, caught between the shadows of uncertainty, wondered whether Arunima hadn't seen him or deliberately chose to ignore him.

Confusion and a hint of hurt lingered within Vihaan as he pondered Arunima's abrupt departure. The bond they shared seemed strong, and he couldn't fathom why she would ignore him. A sense of determination welled up within him, prompting Vihaan to seek answers.

Upon returning home, Vihaan eagerly resumed his playtime with Ahaan, immersing himself in the world of childish joy. As Ahaan drifted into peaceful slumber, Vihaan's mother, displaying a tender touch, began caressing his head. She inquired about his soccer class, and Vihaan enthusiastically shared his day's adventures, including the encounter with Arunima. Perplexed by the unusual story, his mother reassured him, "It's dark, Vihaan. Arunima might not have noticed you."

CHAPTER NINE

Mind Harmony Clinic

The doorbell rang abruptly, and I hastened to open it, finding our neighbor, Dr. Ahuja, and his wife standing at the entrance. Although we had seldom interacted with them before, they now sought our company. After the initial exchange of pleasantries, they engaged in a conversation with my mother.

Curiosity piqued, I excused myself and retired to my room. The murmur of their dialogue floated through the air, occasionally punctuated by my father's arrival. He joined the discussion, and the seriousness of the conversation became evident. Their words carried a weight that I couldn't decipher, leaving me perplexed about the nature of their discussion.

As the discussion unfolded, I heard snippets of dialogues. Dr. Ahuja's voice resonated, "It's crucial to address this sooner rather than later. The symptoms may escalate." My mother's replies were softer, and my father's occasional interjections heightened the sense of urgency.

After what felt like an eternity, the Ahujas bid their farewell, and my parents called me for dinner. The atmosphere in the room was charged, and I couldn't shake off the feeling that something significant had transpired. My inquiries were met with assurances, but the tension lingered in the air, leaving me to grapple with the uncertainty of the situation.

During dinner, my mom couldn't contain her excitement about sharing the events with my dad, especially about Arunima. To my surprise, my dad exhibited a keen interest in every detail I shared. It felt like a bonding moment that had been absent for a long time, and for the first time in ages, I found myself at a loss for more stories to tell. The emptiness left behind was strangely satisfying, signifying a reconnection with my parents.

After dinner, I retreated to my room, but this time, it wasn't solitude; it was a peaceful solitude that allowed me to reflect. I felt compelled to pen down the entire day's events in my diary, capturing the emotional rollercoaster I had experienced.

The following morning, my dad proposed that I skip school for the day and spend time with them. Overjoyed, I readily agreed. In the afternoon, they took me to a place called "Mind Harmony Clinic." Confused, I questioned my dad about the purpose of our visit. He explained that, given everything I had been through, they wanted to ensure my emotional well-being. Dr. Ahuja, the family friend, was also present at the clinic. He called me into his office, where he conducted an assessment of my emotional state and delved into the events of the past few weeks.

Dr. Ahuja's questions were thorough, with a particular focus on the occurrences in the park. His genuine concern and professional demeanor created a space where I felt comfortable opening up about my experiences. It became a session of introspection, unraveling emotions and reflections that had long been buried within me.

CHAPTER TEN

Life is not easy

The clock seemed to slow down during my three-hour conversation at the clinic. A nurse led me to a quiet cabin afterward, offering snacks to soothe my restless thoughts. Meanwhile, my dad engaged in a meeting with Dr. Ahuja.

After what felt like an eternity, my dad returned, and we headed home. Once there, he suggested ordering food from a nearby restaurant, trying to bring a semblance of normalcy to our evening. Following our meal, I retreated to my room, but sleep eluded me. The approaching footsteps disrupted the silence, and I feigned slumber as my parents entered.

Under the cover of darkness, they kissed my forehead, and I overheard my mother's hushed words. "What have we done to him? We're losing him while caring for Ahaan." A solitary tear fell on my forehead, betraying her silent sobs. My heart ached as I grappled with the realization that my mother was crying, and I lay there, unable to offer her comfort.

My father's whispered response sent shivers down my spine. "The need for our love has manifested in Vihaan's creation of Arunima. How can we explain to him that Arunima exists only in his mind now?" The revelation struck me like a physical blow, the nausea rising within me. My mom inquired about Dr. Ahuja's diagnosis, and my dad cautiously mentioned the suspicion of early-stage schizophrenia.

Mom: (whispering with a sigh) Vihaan, our poor Vihaan. (She touches my forehead gently.)

Dad: (softly) We never saw it coming. How did we miss the signs?

Mom: (sitting by the bedside, looking at me) Dr. Ahuja was a godsend. (She glances towards the door to make sure I'm still asleep.) His timely observation in the park, finding Vihaan talking to himself, it made all the difference. We owe him so much.

Dad: (nodding) Yes, we do. (He runs a hand through his hair, visibly troubled.) But what now? How do we navigate this for Vihaan?

Mom: (with a deep breath) How can we explain to him that Arunima exists only in his mind now? (Her voice trembles with a mix of concern and sadness.)

Dad: (leaning in, his expression pained) It's heartbreaking. He believed in her so strongly. How do we break it to him gently without causing more harm?

Mom: (whispering) I don't know, but we need to find a way. He deserves to understand, and we need to support him through this.

In the darkness, I wrestled with the news. Imaginary conversations with Arunima flashed before my eyes. The boundary between reality and imagination blurred, leaving me terrified. As my parents debated whether to talk to me, the weight of their concerns pressed down on me.

Suddenly, my mom's anguished words reverberated, "**Why us?** First Ahaan and now Vihaan! Life is not easy."

The echoes of her despair lingered as I continued to feign sleep, grappling with the profound truth that life had taken an unexpected, challenging turn.

As the haunting question 'Why us?' hung in the air, I lay in the stillness of the night, absorbing the weight of my family's struggle. The realization that life had thrust upon us a journey marked by unforeseen hurdles settled deep within my consciousness. Clinging to the remnants of feigned slumber, I pondered the harsh reality echoed by my mother. The path ahead was uncertain, and the specter of mental health challenges cast a long shadow over our lives. In the silence that followed, I grappled with the profound understanding that, indeed, life was not easy, and the chapters ahead promised both resilience and introspection in equal measure.

www.ingramcontent.com/pod-product-compliance
Lightning Source LLC
Chambersburg PA
CBHW030507170726
47990CB00008BA/3083